Billionaire Romance - Accidentally Flirting with the CEO 4

Billionaire Romance - Flirting with the CEO, Volume 2

Shadonna Richards

Published by Shadonna Richards, 2023.

ACCIDENTALLY FLIRTING WITH THE CEO 4

Shadonna Richards
Copyright 2014 by Shadonna Richards

This book is a work of fiction. The names, characters, places, and incidents are products of the writer's imagination or have been used fictitiously. Any resemblance to persons, living or dead, is entirely coincidental.

ACKNOWLEDGMENTS

Thank you, God, for all my blessings. To my wonderful family and friends for your endless support. And to MDM, MH, Bev, CS and JP, the best editors and beta readers ever! And to all the wonderful readers, I am so eternally grateful to you.

This is a work of fiction. Similarities to real people, places, or events are entirely coincidental.

BILLIONAIRE ROMANCE - ACCIDENTALLY FLIRTING WITH THE CEO 4

First edition. August 4, 2023.

ISBN: 979-8223286882

Written by Shadonna Richards.

Table of Contents

Billionaire Romance - Accidentally Flirting with the CEO 4
(Billionaire Romance - Flirting with the CEO, #2) 1
Chapter 1 3
Chapter 2 20
Chapter 3 22
Chapter 4 33
Chapter 5 41
Chapter 6 47
Chapter 7 51
Chapter 8 53
Chapter 9 57
Chapter 10 62
Chapter 11 67
Chapter 12 73

ACCIDENTALLY FLIRTING WITH THE CEO 4

What happens when your secret fantasies about the hot new CEO are exposed at the office?

Shy, quiet Pamsey Jackson secretly has the hots for her sexy, but emotionally distant, boss Brett Lorenz. But it isn't until she accidentally sends him the wrong digital file (a personal folder with her diary notes and revealing selfies) during a late at night work session for a Valentine's Day ad campaign that things heat up.

The question is: Will things ever be cool between them?

Chapter 1

"Have you ever looked at someone and thought, 'Damn, could you just love me back already?'" – Author Unknown

"We've got a serious problem, guys," Brett Lorenz, Director of Advertising at TLC Advertising Agency, told the account team meeting in the boardroom. "B&B's new *Matchmaking* site changed it up on us again. Their new management team is shifting the direction of their online campaign. They're insisting that we move the deadline to tomorrow by noon to catch Valentine's Day. It's a rush job."

"What?" Luke, the art director said, almost spurting out his Starbucks coffee.

Account Coordinator, Pamsey Jackson froze. She was new to the position and didn't want to start complaining about client workload yet. So she decided to say nothing—for now.

"Are they crazy?" Jim, the copy editor, chimed in. He looked up from his laptop.

"Oh, no. Not again," another member of the account team grumbled.

"We're under a tight deadline, guys. No time for excuses, only *results*," Brett continued, his voice calm yet his tone commanding. Brett had the type of charisma and charm that would make anyone want to do anything for him. He was also an emotionally distant former tech god, who kept everyone at bay.

"But we have that Valentine's Luncheon they're hosting tomorrow. They want us all to be there," Jim said.

Pamsey noticed that Brett flinched at the word *Valentine's*.

She remembered hearing that he hated Valentine's Day. Over the years whenever TLC Advertising held events or dances for Valentine's he would openly voice his disdain for the celebration and talk about how overrated and materialistic it was. But then she'd heard that his ex-fiancée broke off with him on that day. She'd hurt him really bad. No wonder it held bad memories for him. How awful for him to have to work on a Valentine's Day project for a matchmaking services client.

"I know it's last minute, but things move fast in this industry," Brett continued, leaning back in his black leather executive chair in the boardroom, his MacBook opened in front of him. "I'm going to need some of you that work on the B&B account to work overtime tonight. The launch deadline has been moved up to tomorrow, and they're one of our biggest clients."

Pamsey sat opposite Brett around the oak table with her laptop in front of her, taking notes as she tried not to stare at his shapely lips as they moved. God, it was so hard to tear her gaze from his sexy lips.

Not only was he the most helpful guy she'd ever met when she first started working at TLC and when he worked as tech support, but he'd stayed back late to save her butt many times when she'd had mishaps with her computer and almost lost a day's worth of client's work. But he barely spoke to her, except for monosyllabic words.

Still, the man was gorgeous. Too handsome for his own good, what with his dark, handsome features, chiseled cheekbones and dark slicked back hair. *Yummy*. His Brioni Italian-designed dark gray suit complemented his electrifying blue eyes. He looked like a strikingly gorgeous mix of Italian and Spanish heritage. Tall, dark and sexy as sin.

Pamsey was surreptitiously infatuated with him, but she had to keep herself in check. She was on a hiatus from men after the man she was about to marry got his secretary pregnant and ditched Pamsey to marry her instead. And before that, her other ex, her high school boyfriend had been emotionally abusive towards her.

She didn't believe in true love or that she'd ever find a soul mate, either. She just accepted that she was one of the unlucky in love girls out there.

She remembered what her grandma used to say about counting your blessings, not your sorrows. She was grateful that she woke up this morning. Grateful that she was alive. Grateful that she had a roof over her head, though she was behind on rent due to her mother's medical expenses. And she was grateful for having a damn good job in this ad agency considering the state of the economy. So what if she'd end up alone? That was just life.

Still, a little fantasy couldn't hurt, right? Besides, TLC had a strict no dating policy and she needed this job badly. She was the sole caregiver for her ailing mother.

What was it about Brett that drew her in like a magnet?

Was it his smooth, perfectly toned dark skin with the chiseled cheekbones and beautiful blue eyes framed by thick black lashes?

Pamsey didn't know how she would contain her feelings around Brett. He was stunning. When she was working at reception, she would steal glances of him as he walked through the double glass doors with his briefcase and often talking on his cell phone discussing business. She couldn't help but lick her lips.

The sweet scent of his musky cologne always got her going. He was positively breathtaking. And she did not fuss over just any guy like that. It just wasn't like her.

Anyone could catch her eye, but it took a special person to catch her heart. Underneath that hot exterior, he had a heart of gold. He wasn't a dog like some men she'd met. He treated women respectfully from what she'd seen and heard about him. His problem was that he kept a distance from everyone including her. He would praise her work whenever she'd created an impressive ad campaign—though Lisee and her posse would make snarky remarks. She hoped one day to move her way up to creative director.

Before she'd been promoted, Pamsey had been known as the odd receptionist, some mistaking her for Goth since she loved to wear black a lot and her nail polish and hair were jet black. But that was because she often felt like black was befitting of her mood. She just wanted to do her own thing.

But when Brett took over from IT Geek god to Chief Executive Office of Advertising, everything changed in a heartbeat. There'd been drastic changes in account management and clientele portfolio. The agency went through a whole shift.

Suddenly, she found herself going into stores buying clothes she never thought she'd be buying. Well, of course, she would be meeting clients now. She couldn't just come to work in black jeans and black T-shirts or baggy sweaters. She'd charged over $2,300 on her credit card for this new account position. It was important to *look* the part in a prestigious ad agency like TLC—especially working directly with high-end clientele.

And oh, Brett.

She was finally working up close with Brett—not that he seemed to notice her much. In an office next to his, she was seeing him up close and personal as they discussed account matters. And yes, she wanted to impress him. That bugged her more than anything.

She'd never met a man she'd cared much about impressing.

The man dominated her fantasies. She'd often visualize what it would be like to be alone with him—at night. She wondered if his skin was as silky and smooth as it looked. She wondered how his strong arms and hands would feel like caressing her body. What kind of lover was he? Excellent, judging by his tall figure and broad shoulders and the fact that he, like the other execs, worked out at the gym in the basement of the building, pumping iron every day on his lunch break. He walked like a man with stamina, swift and energetic.

His sexual aura was overwhelming. And the funny thing was, he didn't even realize what effect he was having on her.

Then a thought crossed her mind: *TLC Advertising Agency Policy #17.1.1: Dating clients and co-workers is not encouraged and is a conflict of interest.*

The policy had something to do with dating co-workers and how that could have an adverse effect on work, especially if it turned sour. Look what almost happened to Alexa, her former colleague, who ended up marrying one of the founding members and the CEO. Both Alexa and Jess almost faced losing their positions at TLC Advertising, especially under the scrutinizing watchful eyes of HR Director and co-founder Lee, the L in TLC Advertising. Pamsey could not afford to lose this job. No guy was worth that in her books.

Inwardly, Pamsey flinched at the thought of Lee getting wind of her attraction to Brett.

"I can work late," Lisee from marketing chimed in.

"Me, too, boss," Clarence added. "Count me in."

Everyone's eyes suddenly turned to Pamsey's direction. Everyone, meaning office bully Lisee and her clique.

Oh, hell.

They knew it was difficult for Pamsey. She had responsibilities at home.

She had to relieve the caregiver for her mother who now lived with her. Her mother suffered from a severe form of dementia. She could not be left alone. And it was getting difficult to pay the caregiver for overtime. She could not afford that—even with a raise from her new position at TLC.

When Pamsey was at work, it was the only break she really had. But she could only afford to pay so much in a day for someone to relieve her.

In short, Pamsey had no life. But she never got into details about her private life with anyone at work, though Brett was aware of the situation at home given that he was now her boss.

The truth was, Pamsey was not going to send her mother to a nursing home. No way in hell. People with dementia who have a rare gene could develop symptoms as early as their forties. The thought paralyzed Pamsey.

She knew she could be at risk one day if she weren't careful, as some forms of dementia were hereditary. She was always reading books and writing in her journals to keep her mind active.

A page a day keeps dementia away; she'd read somewhere.

By five o'clock, Pamsey had to be out of there. But she was a hard worker. She was always on time, and she worked her butt off. Brett already hooked her up with her offsite login so that she could access her account from home should she need to work from home.

"I...I won't be able to stay at the office," Pamsey said, "but I can work from home tonight." Pamsey swallowed a gigantic lump in her throat, hoping no one in the boardroom would sense her uneasiness.

Lisee rolled her eyes, "As usual," she muttered under her breath. Her friend, Cleo, who worked on the Strausmann Brokers account, stifled a laugh.

That was pretty much Lisee's personality. She was always taking jabs at people or always had something snarky to say. She must not have had a balanced childhood, Pamsey thought.

Most people tried to be sweet as pie to Lisee and join in on her gossip sessions hoping they would not be her next victim—which was foolish really. As the Spanish proverb stated: *Those who gossip to you will gossip about you.*

Pamsey couldn't give two rats who liked her in the office from who didn't. She just did her job and was respectful to everyone. *Haters gonna hate, no matter what you do.*

Her daily motivation mantra helped keep her together in an office charged with politics.

"That's fine, Pamsey," Brett's smooth, silky voice cut through her daydream, though he didn't look at Pamsey. "You can work from home."

Lisee, of course, snickered. Pamsey ignored her hate stare and her attitude. She was glad everyone else did, too. Brett's expression was stone serious when Lisee snickered. He looked as if he was about to say something that would shut her up then he turned back to his agenda. He was clearly not impressed by Lisee's tactics.

"Anything else?" Brett's tone was serious, yet deep and delightful to her ears and stirred a delicious reaction inside Pamsey's body. What was it about his rich voice that struck a chord with her?

When no one else had anything more to add to the B&B agenda, he keyed in some information on his laptop. "Good. We'd better get started on our assignments," he said.

Pamsey felt her inner thighs tingle.

Damn it.

What she would love to do was work from Brett's home. From *his* bedroom.

Stop that, Pamsey. Stop that nonsense, girl. Focus on work. Brett's off limits. Not to mention the mere fact that he doesn't know I exist—beyond work-related assignments.

She really needed to get a life—and a man. When was the last time she'd dated? Like two years ago. Too long since her heart had been betrayed by Caleb, her ex-fiancé.

They'd been friends from college. And what a guy he turned out to be. Let's just say there were too many baby mamas going on with Caleb. He seemed okay at first and told her that he wasn't playing around on her. She should have known. But he had been there for her when she was going through a difficult period in her life. She'd never felt like she fitted in anywhere and well, Caleb, she thought was the one. The smooth talker. The always-knew-what-to-say-to-get-her-going type of guy. Well, she would never trust another guy after that. He'd gotten a job as a sales manager and got his assistant pregnant and married her instead. He'd broken off their engagement on Twitter. She'd had invitations sent out, too, and ended up losing the deposit—most of her savings—on the hall.

For a good while, she'd kept to herself and rarely spoke to anyone. Bad mistake, which she realized now. Still, she would never again open up herself to a man like that again.

She would keep her fantasies about Brett a secret—indefinitely. It was way safer that way. Not to mention she had no choice given the office policy on dating in the workplace. She couldn't afford to be fired for violating that policy.

And as for Caleb, so much for giving a man her heart. That would be the last time she'd let someone into her heart. The truth was, Pamsey grew depressed after that and closed off into her own world. She didn't go out much and wore black even more. People thought she was odd. Different. Well, different was okay in Pamsey's books. At least she wasn't a backstabber who'd cheat on someone they were engaged to.

Focus on work, Pamsey.

That's all in the past now. The past is dead and gone. Stop bringing it back to life. Bury your burdens and keep them buried.

"Now, as you all know we're pressed for time. The new Valentine's Day ad must go live by six o'clock tomorrow evening."

"They're asking for a lot in a short space of time, boss," Pamsey said, before biting down on her lip. Why did she blurt that out?

"Afraid of a little work, Pamsey?" Lisee commented, rolling her eyes. "Or maybe you didn't read the job description where it says you have to be able to work under pressure and under tight deadlines."

"Excuse me?" Pamsey said, arching her brow.

"Pamsey's right," Brett agreed and came to Pamsey's defense to Lisee's surprise.

Lisee's jaw fell open.

B&B had been nothing but a royal pain in the butt since they'd become a client of TLC Advertising agency. They were always paying late, changing deadlines and proposing the most outlandish campaigns—only to scrap it at the last minute after all the hard work had been done by the agency. So much for all those late nights at work on their projects.

"It wouldn't be the first time B&B pulled a last minute switch on us after hyping us up for one of their campaigns," Brett continued, leaning back in the leather chair, his sexy blue eyes had an intent gaze. "Still, we're hired to do a job. We'll get it done on time. We'll do our part. What have you got so far, Luke?" Brett turned his attention to one of the art directors.

"Well, we're still working on the TV clip for the commercial. And we still have another shoot to go. We should be in editing soon."

"You don't have the piece in editing yet?"

"No. Not yet. Remember we had trouble getting that actor B&B requested?" Luke reminded Brett.

"Right," Brett said, looking distracted. He didn't seem himself this morning. "Pamsey?" Brett then asked, turning his attention to her.

"Yes."

"What have you got so far with the print ad?"

"Well, I have three different layouts I'm working on right now," Pamsey said, trying to hide the fluttering in her chest. She felt her heart race a mile a minute. What was it about Brett that made her so nervous? She hated that he was gazing intently at her right now. His sexy eyes penetrated her like warm rays of the sun.

"I'm working on the JiJi shot," Pamsey said.

JiJi was the recording artist who agreed to do a cameo and appear in B&B's upcoming ad campaign.

"I have a shot of her from the studio photo shoot we did a while back," Pamsey continued. "I'm going to Photoshop her in a beach scene with the B&B logo and their new slogan which is the title of her hit song *Match Made in Heaven.*' As you know, a rep from B&B didn't like the original photo shoot and asked that JiJi does one on the beach. Well, she's on tour right now, I figured Photoshopping her in would be more feasible and realistic given the new deadline."

"Good," Brett said, his expression unreadable. Pamsey hated when he did that. The one-word answers. The stern voice. "But I'll need to see it first thing in the morning—latest," he added, a hint of annoyance in his silky, deep voice.

She could tell he was probably not impressed that she could not work late tonight at the office like the rest of the account team. In advertising, it was an unwritten rule that you didn't leave the office until the work was done.

She remembered when Lee placed the ad for her position in the industry magazine. The last sentence in that ad right before the deadline for resume submission was *"clock-watchers need not apply as we are a very busy agency."*

"I'll have it done tonight and email it to you from home."

"Please do that. I'll be working here late tonight," Brett added, his tone softened a fraction—so much that it stirred another round of reaction inside Pamsey. His voice softened like melted caramel.

Oh, how she wished she could be working late at the office alone with Brett. Just the two of them.

"Yeah, working late as the rest of us," Lisee added in, taking another jibe at Pamsey.

Ugh.

Brett ignored Lisee's comment and continued to tap away on his computer.

Pamsey resisted the urge to roll her eyes. She was not going to stare or give Lisee the satisfaction, but boy, some people really had a talent for getting under other people's skins.

Just then, Lee poked her head in. "Did you tell the team?" she asked Brett.

"Tell them what?" he said, firmly, looking up from his MacBook.

"About the supply issues."

"Really, Lee, we have more pressing issues. It's all a billable expense."

Lee frowned. "Before anyone leaves here, I'm just letting you know that we will be implementing new strategies to monitor supplies."

"Monitor supplies?" Pamsey asked, incredulously.

"Yes," Lee said. "I've noticed that the costs of supplies have quadrupled in the last few months alone. It appears that someone or some *ones* have been either using excess supplies or stocking them."

"Are you seriously accusing one of us of stealing supplies from the company?" Lisee said as she rolled her eyes.

Didn't Lee have a life? Were things so bad that she had to baby a group of professional adults and monitor each and every little penny spent on supplies? Good grief.

"You've all been warned. I will be keeping inventory. And I will do what I can to monitor to make sure we don't go overboard on unnecessary spending." With those words, Lee left the boardroom, but not before giving Pamsey a look.

Pamsey tried to ignore it.

But why on earth did she feel as if everybody hated on her this morning? Was it because she had to leave on time every day at five o'clock to relieve her mother's support worker, while everybody else worked late? She still managed to get her client work done.

She was all too aware that if management didn't like a person they would use any little excuse they could to harass or get rid of you.

She swallowed a hard lump. She was always crossing her T's and dotting her I's so to speak. God, it was hard working in a hostile work environment, and if she didn't have Brett to fantasize about now and then, she'd probably have lost it already.

* * *

"Oh, and Pamsey," Brett called after her before she walked out of the boardroom. It was just the two of them in there now.

"Yes," she said, almost breathless. Why did she always get that way around Brett?

"I really will need that print ad tonight and the copy for the announcement." His voice was sharp but a bit husky. What was that about?

"Well, Brett. I did say I would get it done." She tried hard to sound as polite as she could, but she sounded more patronizing than she'd intended.

"You've said a lot of things in the past few months, Pamsey." His expression was unreadable, his tone of voice reserved.

"Excuse me?" Her tummy tickled with butterflies. She felt a surge of heat rise through her.

"The Curoski Account?"

"Oh, that."

"D'Ante Industries."

"Okay," she said, swallowing hard. She'd slipped up, hadn't she? It was the first time in like forever. Pamsey had always been on the mark. In fact, Lee had wanted to fire her then, but she'd later found out that Brett had covered for her and dismissed any claim that Pamsey had been slacking off.

Pamsey's mother had a bout of terrible flare-ups and episodes with her dementia. So much was going on in her private life, but she didn't want to bring it to work. On a few occasions when she'd been up all night at the hospital with her mother, she'd gotten maybe one hour sleep before coming into work. Brett was annoyed as hell and even called her out on it. She'd told him it was personal and didn't want to get into it. Brett accepted her reason for tardiness and missed shifts but Lee did not.

"Listen," Brett's tone softened. "I know you have a lot on your plate. I shouldn't have mentioned those accounts without mentioning the Peg Industries account or the Softmore account. You really saved TLC there. Your ideas were brilliant for their new campaigns. Innovative. You have a special gift with creative concepts, Pamsey."

"Thank you." Her heart thumped hard in her chest.

Pamsey then stifled a yawn. Darn it. The sleepiness was creeping down on her.

"It's morning. Are you tired already? Not enough sleep last night?"

"Sorry, my...my mother was up all night. I was taking care of her."

"Sorry to hear that."

"That's okay."

"I know it's not my business to say but just remember to get enough sleep. Take care of yourself."

Pamsey was stunned into silence. Well, that was a first. Brett barely spoke to her about her personal life or in long sentences.

"I'll try."

"Seriously. You're a valuable member of this team. But if you break down, you're not like our copier machines or computers."

"Yeah, I get it."

"I don't think you do, Pamsey. Unlike our office equipment, your life doesn't come with a warranty. It's not replaceable. You've only got one. Take good care of it."

Whoa. Well, talk about deep philosophy.

"Besides, I need you for that Kalinsky account," his tone changed as if he felt uncomfortable with this conversation. "They really like your work. I don't want you yawning when they get here."

Okay, so his aloofness was back.

He seemed to hesitate for a moment. He walked over to her. She had her files clung to her chest; her nose caught the sweet scent of his delicious aftershave. Oh, Brett-too-sexy-for-his-own-good. He was killing her. Why did he have to be so damn annoying and attractive at the same time?

His beautiful eyes, blue as the summer sky, gazed intently into hers. It was the first time he'd done that. The underlying sensuality of his look captivated her. Brett rarely made eye contact with her. Was something going to happen between them? She felt her inner thighs pulse hard.

Damn it!

Pamsey, you're at work. You're in the boardroom for heaven's sake. And you know Brett's not into you. Stop imagining things. Besides, there's a workplace policy against these things.

Was he going to say something else? Her appraisal was coming up soon. Brett was on the board and would be evaluating her and possibly recommending her for a promotion.

The thought overwhelmed her. Her limbs suddenly felt weak. Then he broke off his gaze. As if realizing he'd made an error in judgment, he shifted his focus to his cell phone and he scrolled down the screen.

"I'm going to send you my notes again on the Kalinksy contract. They'll be in later this afternoon. Type it up. And this time send it to me right away. Understand?" Brett spoke with cool authority. So cool, she shivered under the iciness of his masculinity.

Just then she dropped the files on the floor. She bent down to pick them up, but Brett beat her to it. They'd leaned down together to pick up the papers. His fingers brushed hers and electricity pulsed through her body.

The silky touch of his skin on hers made her tremble with delight.

Crap.

Had she ever gotten that close to Brett where they accidentally brushed against each other skin to skin? Brett had always been distant. As if he were allergic to her or something. And the feeling was delicious. She hated herself for wanting him to touch her again. Did he not feel anything, too? One quick look at his handsome face, told her 'hell no.'

"You'll need to be more careful with those confidential files," he spoke in a clipped voice that forbade any more conversation as he handed her the documents before walking out of the boardroom.

Chapter 2

Brett sat at his desk in the office. It was already late at night, and the rest of the team had just left shortly after seven thirty. The department was quiet except for the sound of office machines still on and the humming sound of the ventilation system.

Was he going crazy? All he kept thinking about was Pamsey Jackson. He'd better get his mind off her. Oh, right. He was supposed to be waiting for an email from her along with the attachment for the ad campaign images.

"You still here, bro?" His brother Travis poked his head in his office at the door. His brother now worked for TLC Advertising—doing some consulting work.

"Still here."

"Hey, you going to the B&B's Valentine's Luncheon tomorrow?"

"You know how I feel about Valentine's Day. It's an overrated bogus holiday that needs to disappear. It programs people to believe that giving and receiving material gifts are more important than true love."

"Damn! Did Cupid stab you with one of his arrows in the wrong place?"

Brett couldn't help but grin. "Sorry, bro. I'm just not feeling it right now. You know how I feel about that...day."

"Oh, right. I should be the one to apologize. I almost forgot that's when Rhea broke it off, right?"

"Yeah, that too."

"Oh, come on, bro. You can't seriously still be hung up on that? There are other women out there. Nice chicks, too.

Seriously though, she wasn't the right woman for you. I knew it from the get-go. She was way too wild and crazy for you—not trustworthy. You deserve someone much better."

"You know I love the ladies, but I'm not interested in having another relationship right now. Besides, women and I have nothing in common."

Travis rolled his eyes. "Yeah, like men and women ever have anything in common. Anyway, good luck with the campaign. I hear they want to launch their new online ad on the same day, tomorrow. That's really cutting it close."

"Tell me about it."

"Well, don't work too late."

"Hey, I don't have to go home to anyone, so I'm not worried about that."

"Whatever, bro. You never know when you meet the right one, you'll change your mind."

"Somehow I don't see that ever happening."

Chapter 3

Pamsey tucked her mother into bed, pulling the pink duvet blanket over her mom's shoulders just the way her mom always liked it.

Her mother looked so comfortable as she lay asleep, with her silver gray hair braided in one long braid to her side.

She then gave her mom a kiss on the forehead. "Good night, mom. Sleep tight," she whispered.

Her mom then slowly opened her eyes. "Good night, Erica."

Sadness filled Pamsey's heart. "No, mama," she gently said, "I'm Pamsey, remember?" Her voice was soft and warm.

Her mother's memory came and went sometimes. She was glad for the job at TLC and the raise from the new position that made it all possible to keep her mother at home instead of having her in an institution. She was able to afford caregivers to come in to be with her mother while she worked.

"Oh, right, Pamsey. I remember," her mother said, her voice frail. "You married that man, right? Where is he?"

Once again, Pamsey's heart squeezed. "Um...no mama, he's...not here." She didn't have the heart to remind her mother that Caleb had taken off with his assistant and broke off the engagement and that she may very well end up alone since she found it hard to ever trust a man again.

It seemed as if her mother had that stuck in her memory about the wedding that they had all been preparing for. Her mother's health had deteriorated further since that time.

"Well, have a good night, mom. I love you."

"Good night...Erica."

Pamsey's eyes moistened with tears, and she smiled and gave her mom another kiss on the forehead. She turned on the night light at the side of the bed and then left the room, closing the door behind her. She hoped that she wouldn't have to be up too late tonight working on that assignment for B&B.

* * *

Eight o'clock in the evening, Pamsey sat hovered over her laptop in the kitchen. Her neck ached and her shoulders were sore. She'd been trying to get that darn cropping thing to a T with the Photoshop layering tool but it just wasn't happening.

Even though Brett had sent her on that course with the other new account coordinators, she still didn't get it. And now, Brett was expecting the newly revised image in his inbox soon. What was she going to do?

What she would do for a nice massage right now, she thought, stretching her hand over her left shoulder and giving it a good squeeze as if to push out all the tension.

The work on the B&B account wasn't her only source of tension.

Her hormones were out of control. It had been way too long since she'd even dated. And she was always thinking about Brett and it was seriously driving her crazy.

He was like a tune she couldn't get out of her head for the life of her.

Was it because he stirred a reaction in her body like no other man had ever done before? And he never showed the slightest interest in her?

Still, she couldn't get over what he'd said to her earlier about taking care of herself. Damn! That was the longest conversation they'd ever had to that point. And it showed that he cared. Though it didn't last long. He had gotten back to being his distant self again.

Just then the phone rang, and Pamsey jumped. Was it work calling? Because she didn't have a darn thing ready for the print ad. And she felt stupid now for calling Brett and asking him to fix it for her. But she might have to end up doing that.

She read the call display: Alexa Tandon

A smile curled her lips. It was her former colleague, Lex—who was now, miraculously married to the former CEO, Jess Tandon. She thought it was a miracle because they both almost lost their jobs after that fiasco with Jess dating an employee and some fake sexual harassment claim from another employee. Boy, that situation was a whole mess, but she was so glad it worked out for Lex, who knew what a poisonous work environment it could be when rumors started flying at TLC between employees. In fact, Pamsey was probably Alexa's only friend at the office at the time.

"Hey, Lex," Pamsey said, answering the phone.

"Hi, Pamsey. How's it going with the B&B account?" Lex said. She was always still very much involved in client files. In fact, Lex was the one who won the account and suggested Pamsey take over when she left the agency for maternity leave. Now Lex was on an extended leave. She may or may not come back. She'd once told Pamsey she loved motherhood but she really missed the fast-paced work at the office—and adult conversations.

"Oh, it's a pain in the butt, as you can imagine."

Lex laughed. She knew all too well what that was about. "I'm sorry you have to work so late tonight from home. I know they can be a bit difficult with changing deadlines. Lee mentioned that yesterday." Lee was Lex's sister-in-law, as well as the HR director, since she was Jess Tandon's half-sister. Lee didn't get along with any of the female employees in the company and she certainly bucked heads with Lex before, almost costing Jess to choose between his sister and his employee-turned-wife. Especially since he'd been in violation of the code against dating in the workplace. That had been a huge fiasco.

"How is your mother doing?" Lex asked, concerned.

"She's good. She had a rough day but the support worker got her settled just before I came home from work. She's asleep right now."

"Oh, good. I think it's wonderful that you help out with your mother, Pamsey. I also want to see you take time out for yourself, too."

"What's that supposed to mean?"

"When was the last time you went out and had fun?"

Pamsey sighed. "Too long, girlfriend. I'm very happy for you and Jess but not everyone gets lucky to find their soul mate at work."

"Oh, come on. What about...um..."

"Don't say it."

"Brett," Lex said.

"Now what makes you think I'm interested in him?"

"Oh, nothing. It's just that I've seen the way you two look at each other at the agency's socials."

"We do not!"

"Yes, you do, Pamsey."

"Even if we did like each other, which we don't, you know more than I do about the company's policy and Lee, the mighty gate-keeper."

Lex chuckled. "You're right. But I just don't want to see you miss out on happiness. You deserve it Pamsey. I remember when you were there for me when all that crap happened at the office."

"I know. Glad you're okay, girl."

"And Pamsey, if I forgot to mention it before...thank you."

"For what?"

"For being a good colleague and never talking about me like the others did. You stuck up for me and I really appreciate it. I don't know what I would have done if everyone had turned against me."

"Don't mention it, Lex. Just take care of yourself and your little one."

"And, Pamsey," Lex seemed to hesitate.

"What is it, girl?"

"I shouldn't tell you this because TLC has that strict policy on dating co-workers in the workplace, but..."

"But what?"

"I think Brett likes you."

"What?"

"I think he does."

"What makes you think that? And what exactly do you mean by like?" Pamsey's heartbeat thumped hard in her throat. Brett liked her? Yeah, right. Not in this lifetime.

"Well, he's always talking about you to Jess—about how wonderful your work is."

"He is?" Pamsey felt her heart explode in her chest. Brett talked about how wonderful her work was to Jess? She was flattered considering she'd had some mishaps in the office thanks to tech issues. Was Lex playing with her mind? But then again, why on earth would Lex call her to tell her this?

Brett had saved her butt one too many times when the computer systems kept going haywire on her. She'd lost files on the system and he'd recover them in no time. There was something sexy about a man who knew his way around technology.

He'd even helped her to figure out how to store stuff on her cloud system from her iPhone in the past.

And talk about cloud storage. She was able to set up her own files now. She put her diary on the computer—because a girl's got to vent about her day to someone—or something. And she'd downloaded her pictures. She often took nature shots, but no one really knew about that. It was a secret hobby she enjoyed. She had also taken some selfies.

She'd saved them on the file but now she was beginning to rethink that. Nothing kinky, just when she was having her breast examination, she'd discovered a little bump that turned out to be nothing. But she'd taken some shots to look at the symmetry and to analyze her body.

And she'd been trying to take butt shots in her new hugging pencil skirts to see if her pencil skirt was too tight for the office.

Then, there was that nice pair of lingerie she'd treated herself to. Since she'd lost quite a bit of weight, twenty-two pounds to be exact, she was proud of herself. She'd really curbed her diet. She didn't normally buy sexy thongs and what have you but she did then to celebrate her weight loss success—not that anyone would ever see her in her thong lingerie, so what did she do? Took a few selfies in the bathroom in front of her full-length mirror to see just how she looked. That was the only way she'd see how her bum with a lacy piece of silk string between her butt cheeks would look from the rear view—should she ever wear it if she ever met the right guy.

Embarrassing photos that she was thinking of now erasing after reading about that scandal where a hacker hacked into some celebrity accounts and posted nude pics of them online. She cringed at the thought.

With the cordless phone still pressed to her ear, she glanced at the file folder with all her personal stuff that was saved to her computer desktop screen. Brett had warned her about saving files on her desktop but she couldn't help herself. It was easier to retrieve.

"Listen, I know when a guy likes me, Lex," Pamsey said, wearily as she moved her cursor over the image on the screen to re-crop it. She was finally making some headway with the photo for the ad campaign.

"Pamsey, you realize that not all guys are the same. We've both known Brett for many years since he started."

"Yeah, I know."

"Well, when was he ever the talkative type? Some guys are just shy."

"Shy?" Pamsey sounded dubious. "I wouldn't call Brett shy."

"He's a tech savvy geek," Lex said.

"Look," Pamsey continued. "I realize I haven't been exactly warm and friendly to him, either. I mean, he's now my boss and trust me, I do think he's hot but I can't figure that guy out. And since there's a policy against dating co-workers, my hands are tied, which is just as well since I need to take a break from relationships. Besides, he's annoying sometimes."

"Annoying?"

"Yes, sometimes, he doesn't make eye-contact, he barely speaks to me, and he just avoids having conversations with me about clients. He's always emailing me even though my office cubicle is right outside his office. What's up with that?"

Lex laughed. "I will say one thing. He's a decent guy."

The word decent stirred Pamsey's heart. Lex was right. When she thought about her smooth-talking ex, Caleb, who got his assistant pregnant then broke off his engagement with Pamsey to marry her instead, Brett seemed more normal by the second.

Pamsey glanced at the time. She'd been talking to Lex for a half hour. "Oh, God. I have to get this thing in to Brett. He's at the office now. Gotta go, girl."

"Good luck."

"Thanks. I think you've been good luck."

"What's that supposed to mean?"

"As we've been talking, I finally got that image cropped and placed on the right background. I'm sending the file now."

"Good for you. Let me know if you need any help with their account."

"Thanks, Lex. I've got it covered."

Pamsey hung up the phone and opened up her email program. She typed in a few words to Brett while her tummy tickled with butterflies.

Brett liked her?

Her heart galloped like a racehorse.

Brett liked her?

He'd been asking about her?

A warm smile curled Pamsey's lips.

Thankfully, her mother had just gone to sleep—earlier than usual tonight. Pamsey was grateful for a little moment of peace so that she could get some work done.

She'd just poured herself a cup of decaf. She had a cup of coffee on the table beside her and a half-eaten ham, lettuce and tomato sandwich—which was now never going to be finished. She couldn't think, or eat. Heck, please don't say she was in love. She could not be. Sure she'd known Brett for years and harbored a sweet crush on his sexy geekiness, but love? No. She liked the guy, a lot, but she couldn't possibly be in love with him. And as much Lex tried to tell her that Brett liked her. She just couldn't get her hopes up. It would hurt too much if her hopes came crashing down from a high distance. Besides, they couldn't violate the TLC's office policy on dating.

Darn that policy.

To Brett,

Here are the files you've been waiting for.

The folder attached contains the three cropped and

*manipulated images for the print ad and some files
for the B&B announcement that will go with the print
ad.*

I did the copy for the announcement in Microsoft Word.

Hope that helps.

Pamsey

Pamsey then cc'd a copy of the email to Luke, Lisee, Jess, Chad, Crato and the rest of the team. And of course to Miss Lee, the HR director. Lee also liked to see what every body was up to. And right now since Lisee and some others have tried to put

Pamsey down by lying that she hadn't been doing her share of work, she wanted to make sure Lee saw how much she'd put in herself. Pamsey was up for an appraisal with Lee and the other directors soon.

She attached the file and hit send.

Your email has been sent, the confirmation at the bottom of her screen read.

Good.

Pamsey then went into the sent folder to get that email to print off the page so that she had it in her records that it was sent to Brett and the team. She grabbed her cup of coffee and took a deep, relaxing sip.

When she opened the sent letter, she almost choked then spurted out her coffee over the computer screen and the keyboard.

File attached: PPF

The hairs stood up on her arms. She stopped breathing.

What the f—-!

PPF? It should have read TLC! That was the file she'd meant to attach, not PPF!

PPF was Pamsey's Personal Folder. It was attached to the email sent to Brett *and the team*. The folder with all her nude selfies and her....oh, God! Her personal diary!

Fuck. Fuck. Fuck.

Pamsey felt her heart explode in her chest. She felt a crushing pain ripple through her body that almost crippled her. She froze, gripped in terror and dazed in confusion. Her eyes were wide with shock as she glared at the computer screen.

How the hell did she manage to attach the wrong file from her desktop to the email? Fuck!

Oh, God! Please no. This can't be happening.

This can't be happening.

But it did happen. It had already happened. And it was too late to do anything about it now.

She'd just sent her most personal folder, not just a file, but a whole folder with revealing images of herself and private thoughts about everyone in her life to Brett...and the *entire* team at TLC Advertising!

Chapter 4

Brett leaned back in his leather chair in his office late at night mulling over some data for the B&B account. Not only was he assigned as the account director for this client but he'd always been their I.T. Consultant as part of a special service provided by TLC Advertising Agency for select clients. Information Tech was his baby. He'd always been a tech geek in college. It was his thing. Figuring out complex formulas and fixing kinks in software systems.

And speaking of kinks. He really needed to keep his mind off sweet Pamsey Jackson or he could kiss his career at TLC goodbye.

Still, she was looking fine these days. Not that she wasn't pretty before. But those legs. What was with those beautiful long, slender exposed legs? When she'd begun working for TLC, she was all black leggings and long floor-length skirts, black baggy sweaters, black nail polish, thick black eyeliner and blue hair or whatever color she was streaking it that month.

But now?

A surge of heat drove through him just picturing her. Hell, he was on fire, just thinking about her.

Her sexiness captivated him. But there was a strict policy on dating in the workplace at TLC Advertising. He wasn't about to risk his new position. Besides, he couldn't' trust women again after what his ex did to him—the woman he was supposed to have married. He could figure out computer codes but the inner workings of a woman's mind were a mystery to him.

Just then a ping sounded from his computer.

New Message from Pamsey.

Brett's groin twitched. A smile crept on his face. He was getting aroused by the word Pamsey on the screen. Why did he just react to her name that way? He really had to get a life—and get laid, so he wasn't always getting aroused by just thinking about Pamsey.

Workplace romance was forbidden at TLC.

Besides, most of the women he knew weren't attracted to men who were geeks.

He could see she had sent a file attachment with the email she'd sent in the preview window. A grin curled his lips.

Good girl.

She'd done her job. He felt bad she had to work from home late, knowing her obligations. He admired the fact that she kept her mother at her place and decided to care for her herself instead of sending her to a nursing home. He knew it must be incredibly difficult for her, not to mention hard as hell on her social life.

Still, she was an employee and he was her boss. So he knew he had to strike any ideas out of his head of anything ever happening between them. Ever.

Yet, he noticed her gaping at him earlier in the boardroom today. What the hell was that about? She could barely keep her mouth closed when he stood up and spoke by the overhead projector.

God, he wondered what her lips would feel like on his. They looked so silky and plump, kissable.

His groin reacted just now thinking about her.

Stop that, Brett. Focus. She's an employee. You're her boss.

He remembered all too well what went down with Jess and Alexa when they'd started dating surreptitiously. But oh, Lee wasn't having any of it. Lee would fry him if she even found out what kind of thoughts he was having about his account coordinator. Not that he cared much what Lee thought, but he knew Lee would go after Pamsey next. And he didn't want her job to get screwed up for anything like breaking the office dating rules.

Just then Jess called.

Speak of the devil. "Jess," Brett answered.

"Hey, you're still working on the B&B?"

"Like crazy. There's a lot of stuff not making sense in their database."

"Anything suspicious?"

"Like a virus? I don't think so. But I'm not ruling that out just yet."

"What about their campaign?"

"Yes, their big transformational campaign," Brett said. "Well, it's coming along. Pamsey just sent in the ad copy and the notes. I'm confident she's got it all together. We can all go through it in the boardroom tomorrow and see what each of us have at the same time."

"Good. Good going, Brett. This one is huge."

"You don't have to tell me that."

"So glad we have you on board and especially in the IT role."

"Don't mention it."

"Have you heard of the Banque de Lux?"

"Yeah, it's some new private bank in Europe, right? Holland, I think. Why?"

"Well, for some reason, they've been linked to B&B's account. And B&B is transferring large amounts of money there."

"Why should we care where they choose to channel their profits?"

"We shouldn't."

"Oh, I get it. Tax implications. You think they're trying to avoid taxes."

"Listen, forget I even mentioned it, Jess. It's all good. I just don't think it's wise for them to invest their profits in such a new organization that doesn't even have a proven track record. But hey, it's their call, right? It's their money."

"Yeah, I guess," Jess said. Brett could hear the sound of a child playing in the background. "Just as long as we make sure our campaign brings them to the next level in their product launch, we've done our part. We're good to go." Jess paused for a moment, then spoke. "Who else will be coming to the meeting tomorrow?"

"The marketing director from B&B, Pamsey, Lisee and the rest of the team, why?"

"Just wondering. I won't be able to make it in tomorrow."

"No worries. I've got you covered, man. By the way, how is Alexa doing—and little Jesse? I heard him just now in the background."

"Great. Can't complain. You know family life has taught me what's important. It's helped me to settle down and enjoy the simple things."

"I'm happy for you, Jess," Brett said.

Then a sinking feeling entered his gut. Why did Brett feel a pang of jealousy? It was crazy. Of course, he was truly happy for Jess. He really was. If anyone deserved happiness, it was his associate. Jess had found the dream love of his life. And Brett had never seen Jess so much happier, so relaxed and content.

Brett drew in a deep breath. It must be nice to have someone to go home to, someone who understood you, who loved you and treasured you no matter what.

Brett wondered if he'd ever find such heaven on earth paradise. Probably not. He wasn't open to relationships anymore. They didn't work out. They never did. Women just weren't honest with him and they came with way too much emotional baggage and drama. He liked his life the way it was. Not tied down. Able to work as late as he had to and not have anyone nagging him.

Mind you, Jess used to work all kinds of hours around the clock until he married Alexa. And now? He couldn't care less about working overtime. He was still passionate about the business but everything worked around his time with his wife.

Brett thought he was in love once.

He admitted now that he might not have been so shrewd in the emotional department. Gadgets and gizmos were his things. He could figure out the most complex tech problems. Women, not so much.

He was keeping his heart under lock and key after what his ex-fiancée, Rhea did to him. In his books, romance wasn't real. He'd given Rhea everything—even a place to stay at his home, and what did she do? Started sneaking around on him.

They'd first met in senior year at high school and later at college, and he'd ended up doing most of her homework for her. He realized now that she'd only been using him. He was the geek and she was the popular girl in school.

They were as different as day and night. Rhea never really understood him. She was a party girl that liked to get around. He was the guy that trusted the wrong woman. While he was busy working late hours at the office, she'd been bringing lovers back to their home.

Why on earth did he even try to make that relationship work? She was shallow and materialistic and was only with him because of his *what* he had, not *who* he was.

Would he ever find a woman who shared the same interests and values as he did?

Well, his ex had found someone else. He'd been away on a six-month trip and when he'd returned, she was already four months pregnant by the time he'd gotten back. He was even willing to forgive her and tried to make the relationship work somehow. Then she had the audacity to break up with him via text messaging. On *Valentine's Day*. She'd found someone with a little more money than he had, apparently—and someone who liked to party as hard as she did.

Brett's thoughts were distracted by a ping on the computer. Lee had already opened Pamsey's email—before he'd even had a chance to see the new print ads and copy for the announcement. *Shit*! Lee wasn't even working directly on the account. Why was she so eager to always look in on Pamsey's work?

He'd be willing to bet she was spying on Pamsey. She'd mentioned that she didn't think Pamsey was working up to standards, to which Brett had fiercely disagreed. Luckily Brett would be in on the employee appraisals and had some say over her job performance. The truth was, Brett kind of liked having Pamsey on the account, though they'd barely spoken.

Lee was always hard on the female employees especially. That woman seriously needed to get a life and get a grip on herself. Brett was all too aware of the stuff that had gone on with Lee's threats against her own brother, Jess and her bullying, in Brett's opinion, of Alexa, who coincidentally was working on the B&B account also, before she took her maternity leave. Well, there was no way in hell Brett was going to let Pamsey go, or intimidate her work, not if he had anything to do with it.

Well, he might as well open up Pamsey's email now.

He read the message and then he clicked on the attachment. It was a file labeled PPF. What the hell did PPF stand for? Shouldn't it be TLC? He'd received attachments from her when she'd worked from home in the past. The files were usually marked TLC.

He didn't think much of it at the time. He leaned back in the leather seat and casually crossed his leg, putting his foot on the opposite knee. He put his pen to his chin and hit the download button on the attachment. It was taking a long time to download.

For *three* pictures?

Just then Brett, puzzled beyond comprehension, looked on the file size. That was a damn big file size for three photo images.

He waited patiently.

Two minutes to download, the icon on the screen read.

Two minutes to download? Download what? Three photo images? The system at TLC Advertising was pretty state-of-the-art. They used the latest software programs and the speediest processors in their newly purchased computers throughout the entire firm. It didn't make any sense why it was taking forever for three photos to get downloaded to his computer. He'd scanned the system for viruses already. In fact, he had the auto program do that every day in case any of the employees accidentally downloaded any phishing or spyware or other viruses that have known to crash other company's entire system or compromise their database. That was never going to happen to TLC, not while he was around.

Just how many pictures did Pamsey send? Her entire portfolio? His frustration was growing now. Pamsey had better not have sent infected files.

Download ready, the screen read.

Finally.

There were a few attachments. His gaze followed the icon marked: Photos. There was another file folder marked Brett. That was obviously the assignment for him.

He leaned back in his chair with his foot propped up and loosened his shirt tie before he clicked open the first file.

Chapter 5

Pamsey couldn't help herself. Tears welled in her eyes, stinging her. She glared at the computer screen, in pain and shock. Not to mention humiliation. What was she going to do?

She then got up and went to the window.

Her whole business was out there on the Internet now and soon would be in the minds of all her colleagues—all the haters.

And Brett.

What would he think about her now?

And Lee?

Pamsey knew she needed to find another job now. Lee wouldn't tolerate that kind of explicit stuff at the office. Heck, Lee, the HR queen, didn't even tolerate employees flirting, never mind sending nude pictures to each other, or the board of directors. She'd given her own brother Jess, who was also on the board and Alexa grief when they'd started seeing each other.

TLC had a strict policy about dating and sexual harassment so to speak, especially since not too long ago, the company almost went down with fake claims of harassment by disgruntled former employees.

This was not good.

Not good at all.

She could not breathe right now. It hurt even to draw breath. The tears streamed down her cheeks. Pamsey always tried to keep her private life—well, private. She never got involved in politics at work, never talked about anyone behind their backs, and never revealed too much about herself or her home life. She just pretty much kept to herself and now...everyone was going to know the truth about her. They would see her diary entries, know her fears, her secrets, her desires and know how she felt about Brett.

Hell, Brett was going to think she was some sex-craved stalker—which she was totally not. But from reading her diary entries, one might come to that logical conclusion that she was.

She'd talked about everything in her diary to what she thought about his weird mannerisms when she'd first met him years ago. How she thought he was stuck up and full of himself, then how much she was undyingly in love with him and wished she could mother his kids. She even wrote about how much he made her body tingle in all kinds of places and how he was the one she'd come to when she'd touched herself thinking about him in her bed.

Ugh.

What had she been thinking?

Therapy.

Her online diary was supposed to be therapy. Now it was going to turn out to be a nightmare in hell. Now, she was probably going to need therapy and much, much more.

She remembered the article she'd read about celebrities having their private nude pictures splayed over the Internet after being hacked.

Never, ever in her life would she ever have thought that she, too, could have had her privacy exposed like that, making her so vulnerable—even though, unlike the celebs, this was by her own error.

But how many of her co-workers would do the right thing and just hit the delete button without reading once they opened up the attachment to find out it was the wrong file sent in error?

Human nature would probably kick in. Or was that, curiosity?

Of course, only in a perfect world, would they ever do the right thing.

Her hands trembled; her entire body shook right now. But she mustered up the courage to pick up the phone.

She gazed out the window at the night sky with the stars sprinkled against the darkness. It was a clear night, but too bad her mind wasn't clear right now.

What was she going to do?

Who could she call?

Brett?

Alexa?

The Let's Talk Helpline?

God, she was losing her mind, right now. This was a major crisis. She would never be able to face anyone ever again. Especially not Brett. Oh, heavens, she'd said some horrible, crazy things about him. Then her pictures. What would he think about those? That she was a loser who took nude pics of her butt and oh, God, had a bit of cellulite too. It would have been one thing if she had Photoshopped the natural skin, but oh, no. He would see everything.

She hugged herself, biting down on her lip.

"Hello," Alexa answered the phone.

"Lex," Pamsey was aware how breathless she sounded. Her heart was pounding a mile a minute, but Alexa was the only person she could think of calling at a time like this before heading down to TLC headquarters to break into the office and destroy the company server—not.

"Pamsey?" Alexa sounded alarmed. "What's wrong? Why do you sound like that?"

"Everything's wrong, Lex," Pamsey's voice broke. She was choked with emotion as she told Alexa what just happened since their last phone call.

"Oh, my God! Pamsey that's awful. Are you sure you sent your personal file? The whole thing?"

"Yes. I'm sure. I saw the sent message. It's all there. Oh, Lex. I fucked up badly. Now my whole life is over. And Brett's going to hate me and fire me."

"No. It's not over, Pamsey." Alexa's voice was warm and supportive yet firm. Alexa knew exactly what Pamsey was going through right now. "We can figure this out."

Heck, a couple of years ago, Lexy had tried to get Pamsey to get Brett to help her delete the sexy email she'd sent to Jess by mistake. An emailed romance writing assignment to her classmate and best friend Macy, who now worked at TLC. The assignment was to write a hot love scene, and of course, Lex had named Jess as her hero in the story. Talk about embarrassing. The problem was, at the appraisal meeting Jess had read the email right then and there. Long story short it had been a rocky and terrifying experience that almost cost them both their jobs, but it turned out all right in the end, didn't it? The trouble was, there was no way in hell did Pamsey see how this could possibly turn out all right in the end. Not only would Brett see that email, but so would Lee and everybody at TLC. She was done. She was finished. She was over.

"How can we figure this out, Lex?" Pamsey's voice quivered.

She held a tissue to her nose, sobbing. Her heart squeezed in her chest.

She really liked Brett a lot, and as much as her job was a pain some days, she loved working in the ad industry and at TLC.

"We can get Brett to delete the email, remember? I was trying to get Brett to remove the message I'd sent to Jess from the main server, but the problem was Brett was off that day. He had an appointment. Remember when I came into the office early and asked you where Brett was?"

"I remember it like it was yesterday, Lex. But you're forgetting one thing."

"What?"

"My email was sent to Brett, too. Don't tell me he's not going to be the least bit curious what's in that message. He probably already opened up the attachment."

"Oh, I see your point." Alexa's voice fell.

Pamsey took a deep sigh. "I can always try to get into the office right now and ask security to let me in."

"And then what?"

"I don't know. I wouldn't do anything except try to cancel the email."

"But you know it's impossible. Only an IT savvy person like Brett might know. And even then, most emails can't be retrieved once sent."

"I know," Pamsey groaned.

"You know Pamsey. I think the only thing you can do right now, short of praying, is going to the office and see Brett. Or at least speak to him over the phone. Tell him the truth. Tell him what happened."

"I think you're right, Lex. I'm going there right now. But I've got to call the nursing agency first."

"What? Why?"

"My mother, remember?"

"Oh, right. You poor thing. You have a responsibility as a mother. You're an amazing daughter, Pamsey. I forgot you can't leave her alone there."

"I know. She's asleep but if she wakes and I'm not here. Anyway, I'll see if they can get a health care aid in right away to sit and watch mom."

"Good thinking."

When Pamsey ended her phone call, she called the Nurse Care Agency and asked them to send over a sitter to stay with her mother for a four-hour shift.

It took ages for them to call her back given the time of night and short notice. But they managed to send someone over there soon.

Pamsey had already called the security at TLC to see if Brett or anyone was still in the office. Luckily, she'd made friends with the night time security officer who often worked day shifts, and he'd told her that Brett was still there.

She drew in a deep breath, washed her face, got changed into her street clothes, brushed her hair and grabbed her keys.

She was going into the office that time of night to see whatever the hell she could do.

Pamsey had to face the music.

She had to face Brett.

Chapter 6

When Brett opened up the first emailed file Pamsey had sent him, he leaned forward in disbelief. His entire body stiffened. His jaw was dangerously pressed shut, his heart beat fiercely.

Was this some kind of sick joke?

Why the hell would she send him these notes? What the heck did this have to do with B&B?

His eyes scrolled down the scene of the rambled text with multiple dates attached to various sections like diary notes or journal notes.

Jan 23rd...Brett's a real jerk, plain and simple.

May 4th...He's arrogant and rude....he barely says hi in the morning....always ordering me around....does he not understand the fundamentals of human interaction...I think not...if he'd get his head out of gadgets and look up once in a while...

Today is July 5th....I can't believe he's been promoted...Does he even know the first thing about being a CEO? Why would they make him director....oh, right...he's brought in millions of dollars to the company...he's innovative...creative...brought in high profile clients...drives a fancy car...attracts women clients...still my heart beats for him...I must be really in need of a life if I'm still thinking about this guy day and night....he doesn't know I even exist beyond a few memos...

July 6th...Ooh, I'm going insane...he's wearing Old Spice again. Shit! He's driving me crazy...want to jump his bones...looks too damn fine in his navy blue Armani suit...

July 10th...I can't think when I'm around this guy... The things he does to my brain, to my body...

I can't believe I get off thinking about him. Imagine that? I hate myself for that. I can't believe I came just now...touching myself, thinking about this guy's gorgeous face...Brett is not just hot...he is serious orgasm-inducing-kind-of-hot...

Orgasm-inducing-hot? Just what the hell was that supposed to mean? Was that what she thought of him? He continued to scroll down the text on the screen in disbelief.

...I keep fantasizing about his firm, hot body over me...inside me...wonder if he's a huge as he looks...Am I even his type? Would he do me? Yeah, like that would ever happen in this lifetime...maybe, he's not interested in women...I never see him with a girlfriend...then again, he IS private...and who's to judge...nobody ever sees ME with a man picking me up from work...

But I like so many things about him....the way he solves puzzles...and tech problems...the way he smiles whenever he does...the way he laughs...whenever we're working together.

I can't believe we have some stuff in common. We both love classical music. I never let him know when he mentioned it in a meeting with one of our clients who plays classical music.

Would love to go to the opera with him or symphony.

He mentioned to one of our clients in astronomy that he enjoys watching the stars at night. Imagine that? So do I...it's a chance to appreciate the universe and the miracles out there...

I would steal glances at him when he's not looking...

Does he even notice me?

...boardroom again...he talked a lot today....couldn't stop looking at his lips while he moved them...so, so sexy...wonder about kissing his lips...wondering if he goes down on a woman to give her

pleasure...hmm, I feel hot thinking about that...oh, his girlfriend is one lucky woman...

Brett's lips twitched in disbelief. Was he more amused or more annoyed? He couldn't figure out which emotion fired inside him right now. It was a mixture of both. Normally, Brett didn't care a darn what others thought of him. Not one iota. But this? This was a bit different, he had to admit to himself. Because in spite of himself, he actually had feelings for Pamsey. But right now he was too furious to even go there with those feelings.

She thought he was annoying, huh?

She thought he didn't even notice her?

A grin of amusement curved his lips at her unbelievable thoughts. Was that how women thought? He was getting a peek into Pamsey's mysteriously beautiful mind.

She'd obviously sent him her online diary. He felt sick to his stomach for her. She'd also intimated details of her breakup with her ex. And how it was difficult for her to trust men.

He quickly clicked over to the images folder. Oh, God, please tell him she'd sent the pictures of the new print ad for B&B, their client.

When the images downloaded on his computer screen, Brett could not believe what he was seeing.

A bare butt photo of Pamsey, the reserved, quiet account coordinator filled his screen and instantly made his erection hard.

The photo looked as if she'd taken it in the bathroom, looking into her mirror with the cell phone up taking a shot. He could see the flash. Her bare rounded bottom was naked except for a pink, silky looking thong string sliding down the center. *Oh, God! Help me.* His erection strained so hard it hurt. The photo left little to the imagination, he thought to himself, loosening his silk tie some more.

He had to take a second look.

"You sent your selfies with your email, Pamsey?" Brett murmured to himself.

The girl had a beautiful, curvaceous ass, he admitted. Her skin looked smooth and real, oh God help him—so real, not like those phony airbrushed models. What he would do to be right there between her soft, beautiful legs.

God, his manhood was throbbing now, straining against the fabric of his silk boxers. He had the urge to release himself right there in the office. His phone started to ring. He ignored it. He was too stunned to speak right now. He was aware his breathing was heavier now.

What was Pamsey doing? Teasing the hell out of him? Man, he was having all kinds of emotions rushing through him right now. His face grew hot just salivating over her body so much he had to loosen his silk tie.

Then a thought struck him and made him respond quickly. Before doing anything else, he clicked out of the attachment and saw that she'd cc'd the entire team at TLC Advertising.

Shit!

Chapter 7

Pamsey's heart pounded hard in her chest as she walked into the dark reception area of TLC Advertising, the sound of her heels tapping on the marble floor echoed down the halls. It was late in the middle of the night and it would probably be her last day on the job. Ever.

Brett was going to fire her.

Her co-workers were going to be disgusted with her.

HR was going to kill her.

It was over. Why had she even bothered coming back? Why didn't she just change her identity and move to another state and erase her online accounts?

Because she just couldn't. What would happen to her mother? Who would look after her mom?

What would happen to her relationship with Brett?

She just had to see him. She thought of all those dreadful things she'd written about him. Not to mention details of her breakup with her ex-fiancé. *Crap*!

As she reached the glass door leading towards Brett's office, she froze. She was stunned to see Brett standing there, casually leaning against her desk, outside his office. His arms were folded across his chest.

Her heart fluttered in a panic.

A million thoughts rushed through her mind. This guy probably knew all her secrets by now. He'd probably seen her most revealing pictures of herself. She felt vulnerable. Stripped naked in his eyes, even though she was fully clothed in her short pencil skirt, black cardigan and gray tank top underneath it.

"B-Brett, what are you doing there?" she said, her lips trembling. Her heart throbbed so hard in her chest; she thought she was going to have a heart attack.

"I could ask you the same thing," he said, his silky deep voice was so cold it sent shivers down her spine. "Security informed me that you were on your way up." His dark, sexy eyes penetrated her and she felt the heat of his gaze. Her skin became moist with hotness.

Oh God, he's read the email...

Chapter 8

"You'll never guess what just happened, Jess," Alexa said to her husband. She sat up in the bed, while he lay on his side under the plush duvet covers.

"Lex, it's one o'clock in the morning," he grumbled.

"I know, honey, but I'm worried about Pamsey…and Brett," she added, ignoring Jess's cue. "Jess, wake up."

Jess got up and sighed, he looked adorable with his mousy hair tussled from an hour's sleep. They'd both gone to bed around midnight but Alexa couldn't sleep. She kept tossing and turning. She just felt so…bad for her friend. After all, Pamsey had been there for her through the whole debacle with her and Jess.

"Right. What is it, Lex?"

"It's Pamsey. You remember that sexy email I *accidently* sent to you before we started, you know, dating?"

A grin curled his sexy lips. "Yeah, how can I forget? I read it during your evaluation in the boardroom with the rest of the board members." He propped himself up, sleepy eyed.

She felt terrible for waking her adorable hubby, knowing he had a crazy day ahead of him already. Jess was amazing in every way. He was a great dad who did more than his share of daddy duties in addition to still providing support for the team at TLC, the very agency he co-founded with his sister, Lee, and cousin, Chase. But more importantly, he was her best friend, the best lover ever and the one person she could talk to about anything…

"Okay, now you've got my attention, Lex. What does that email have to do with Pamsey?"

"Well, she sort of sent Brett, something similar."

"What do you mean she sent him something similar?"

"I mean," she said, fidgeting with the silk hemline of the duvet, "she was supposed to send him that file on the B&B account. You know? The print copy and the mock ad with the photo cropped and photoshopped."

"And?"

"Well, she told me when she finished, she did what she usually did when she worked from home as part of the client team. She sent the email attachment in the folder and copied everyone on the team, including Lee."

"And what's wrong with that?"

"Well, what's wrong with that is she sent the wrong file, Jess. Oh, Jess, we have to do something. We have to help her...and Brett."

"Whoa, whoa there. Now, wait a minute. What file are you talking about, Lex?"

"Her *personal* file. She told me she keeps a folder on her desktop near to her work folder and it has her online diary notes, her selfies, her personal documents, her..."

"What?" Jess's eyes widened. Alexa was so glad to have Jess's support and understanding in all of this. It was so nice to have someone who supported you no matter what and who validated your concerns and didn't dismiss your fears or your worries. Jess was all that. She was beyond appreciative that things worked out between Jess and her, despite the alarming statistics on office romances gone wrong. She just hoped that Pamsey's situation would not take a turn for the worse.

"She sent the whole damn file to the office?" Jess sounded incredulous.

"Yes," Alexa said, nodding sorrowfully. "The whole damn thing. Oh, Jess, Lee is going to fire Pamsey and Brett—if she doesn't kill them first."

"She won't," Jess sighed.

"How do you know that?"

"Because, hopefully Brett can do something about it."

"But what if Brett can't do anything about it? Or worse. What if he can do something about it but fires Pamsey himself?"

"He won't."

"How can you be so sure?"

"Because that guy has never liked any girl more than Pamsey."

"But, Pamsey said she said a lot of mean things about Brett in her diary—he won't like her then."

"She did what? Why would she do that?"

Alexa shrugged. "I don't know. I guess maybe, if he had told her how he felt about her...?"

"Whoa, wait a minute. So this is a guy thing now? It's Brett's fault?" he said, arching a brow. Oh, Jess looked so sexy. His lips curled in amusement and astonishment.

"Well, Jess, you know men never say what's on their mind."

"Oh, how so?"

"Well, I had no idea you liked me until..."

"That's different and besides, you didn't let on how you felt about me either."

"That's not true," Alexa protested.

"It's *very* true, Lex."

"Fine, okay," Alexa mumbled.

Jess sighed. "It's too bad. I feel sorry for Pamsey, but we all know we have to *think before we click*. Once we send something into cyberspace, that's it."

He looked at the clock on the display.

"Now when did she send this email?" he asked.

"Not too long ago."

"Chances are, no one will open it until morning, which means—"

"But how can you be sure, Jess?"

"I can't be sure. But let's just hope, Lex. There's nothing more we can do right now. The internet works at lightning speed."

Alexa frowned. "Well, that's no help."

"What more can I say, Lex?"

Alexa folded her arms across her chest. "Don't you think they'd make a cute couple?"

He gave her an incredulous look. "Are you serious?"

"I think if they got together, they'd make the most beautiful babies. They look like they were made to be together."

Jess rolled his eyes and turned off the bedside lamp.

Chapter 9

Brett got up and moved closer to Pamsey. Her pulse raced, her legs felt weak and lifeless.

Then she uttered those words to him, breathlessly: "I'm so s-sorry, Brett."

"You're sorry, huh?" he said in a smooth, dangerously low voice as he neared Pamsey, his hands still shoved in his pants pocket of his expensive-tailored suit. The scent of his sexy cologne tantalized her senses.

Pamsey's breath halted. She could not breathe. Her legs felt weak and unstable. Her heart pounded and her pulse roared in her ears. The flesh between her legs throbbed and moistened.

Oh, Brett. Please, please don't hate me.

The magnetic energy between them was electrifying. So intense, she thought she would die from shock. Her heart quickened so much, she didn't think her body could keep up to compensate for her blood pressure soaring from all this excitement mixed with anxiety.

What was he going to do?

She wanted him. Oh, so badly, the feeling ripped through her veins at lightning speed. She thought she would lose it soon if he didn't touch her, if he didn't make her fantasies come true.

"Y-yes, I'm sorry," she said, breathless. "Y-you read m-my e-mail?"

His lips were close to hers and she was dying for him to take her, right there by her desk where security cameras were probably in clean sight but she didn't care at that moment. She didn't know what got over her but she didn't mind if she were caught on camera right now making out with him.

Brett captured her with his deadly, gorgeous gaze.

"Yes, I did," he said seductively, his voice controlled.

A wicked glint played in the deep ocean-blueness of his eyes. He traced the outline of her jaw with his fingers sending waves of excitement rushing to her loins. She tingled at his soft strokes.

Breathing heavily, he lowered his head to hers, and softly brushed his lips against hers. The heat of his warm lips, as he touched her lips, made her heart leap in her chest.

"Oh," she moaned, with delight. His lips were softer and more delicious than she'd imagined. He stroked her chin with his soft finger and gently tugged her close to him. His other hand slid down her back and she tingled inside. He pulled her closer to him and the moist sweep of his tongue slid between her lips before he kissed her so gently, then passionately, more passionately than she'd ever been kissed before.

Ripples of electricity pulsed through her body. She thought she would die from all the rush of excitement coursing through her blood. His warm flesh devoured hers so sweetly.

Oh, Lord. This guy can really kiss.

The flesh between her legs vibrated. Her panties were moist as sin. She was heightened in her arousal from French kissing Brett. The way he held her firm and lovingly as he passionately kissed her again and again, his lips moving down her skin to her neck as he sucked on the sensitive flesh with his soft warm lips, his warm breath on her skin, his delicious cologne wafting to her nostrils. She was in heaven. She was somewhere else—not on earth.

Dizzying currents raced through her as he held her, her nipples were hard pebbles under her tank top. He slid his hand under her tank top and caressed her breast, then stroked her nipple to pleasure.

"Oh, Brett," she moaned again, unable to control herself, breathing harder and harder and faster and faster. She felt as if she would explode right now if he wasn't inside her soon. Her inner thighs pulsed harder. This was what she'd fantasised about since the day she'd met Brett. She could not believe this was happening. This was a dream. It had to be. Reality never felt so good before.

Magic happened right there. She didn't know where she was or who the heck she was at that moment.

Her head was still tilted back, her eyes closed in ecstasy enjoying the feel of his flesh on hers, but then he stopped, leaving her breathless, lingering. He pulled back, a smug grin on his lips.

"Is that what you were dying to know, Pamsey?" he said in a low sexy voice. "How my lips would feel?"

"What?" she opened her eyes, dazed. "You son of a b—"

"Careful," he lifted his finger to her lips, grinning. "We're still in the office, remember? No profanity will be tolerated as per company policy."

"What? Company *policy*?" she fumed. "What about kissing me? Isn't *that* against company policy, too?"

"You had a question in the email you'd sent me, I just wanted to answer it. You know how much I can be a stickler for answering all questions that are directed to my attention."

Pamsey's chest heaved. She was furious and embarrassed. Okay, so now she knew exactly how he must have felt reading that email she'd sent him.

She was still buzzed from the high of his oh, so sexy kiss. Where in heaven's name did he learn to kiss like that?

She placed her hands on her hips, her brows furrowed.

"Okay, I'm sorry I sent the email. But you're being a j—"

"A jerk, right? Isn't that what you wrote in your December 11th entry?" He arched a brow. He leaned back on her desk, his arms folded across his broad chest. His silk tie was slightly loosened at the neck, she noticed.

"You read that one, too?"

"I have this horrible speed-reading habit. You sent me the message with my name on that folder, so I assumed it was intended for my reading. Unfortunately for you, I could read large amounts of text in a short space of time. But you already know that, don't you? What was that reference you made for me...?" he pretended to ponder, his finger stroking his chin. "Oh, right, an emotionally-detached geek."

"You have some nerve, Brett!" Pamsey felt heat rise to her chest and to her face. She must look as red as a beetroot right about now.

Brett was enjoying this, wasn't he? But if she was honest with herself, she was enjoying being in his company right now, too. She was having a heated discussion with Brett, the one who made her heart race every day while she worked in the office. Well, it was better than their previous monosyllabic discussions.

Brett was the man who'd saved her butt too many times when she'd had weird glitches in her files at work, and when she'd lost that Bricker Account file, he'd stayed all night retrieving it for her and kept it from Lee so she wouldn't get fired.

How could she hate him? But how did he feel after seeing those awful diary posts when she was annoyed with him—or frustrated that she could never get through to him emotionally?

Well, how's this for an emotional breakthrough, Pamsey?

"*I* have some nerve?" he echoed, arching a brow. "Those are your words in that email, Pamsey—not mine." He glanced at his watch. "I think we should go into my office. Now."

Pamsey realized there were still in a public area outside his office. At least there would be no security cameras inside his office.

"Fine," she murmured, her mind still on what happened a moment ago.

What *had* happened?

Brett kissed her.

Oh, God. Brett really kissed her. And his lips felt *so* good! She was trembling with desire for him.

She'd never been kissed like that before. Ever. She didn't know her body could be set aflame from the feel of a man's lips. And how could those lips possibly belong to someone who didn't care?

"And to answer your other question—yes, I do. And I enjoy it very much," he said in a deep sexy voice that slid off his tongue like raw silk. A wicked grin curved his soft lips.

"Y-yes?" she echoed, breathing hard. Her inner thighs throbbed with want and anticipation. Was he admitting that he enjoyed going down on a woman?

Gulp.

Chapter 10

Have mercy.

It was getting hot in there. Too hot. Was Brett referring to pleasuring a woman between her legs?

The very space between Pamsey's thighs ached and throbbed.

Her mind raced thinking of all the things she'd written about him, wondered about him, questioned about him.

He said nothing else after that while. His answer to the unknown question lingered in her mind and shattered her soul. He was driving her crazy.

Brett showed her to the chair opposite his desk, then sat behind his desk with the computer still on. He keyed in some text at a rapid speed and clicked on his mouse a few times.

"What are you doing?" she said, curious, still trying to catch her breath.

"Trying to undo the damage you may have done to yourself and your reputation, Pamsey."

"What?"

"Lucky for you, only one other person, besides myself, opened your email. And that was Lee."

"Oh, no."

"I'll speak to Lee tomorrow and let her know you've sent the wrong file and she must delete without reading. I'm intercepting the other messages on the main server so they don't reach the accounts of the other staff members."

"You can do that?"

"Yes. I programmed the company's internal email system that way."

"Oh, Brett. I...I don't know what to say," she murmured, tearful. Of course, he was trying to help her.

Brett's thoughtful words traveled straight to her heart at that instant, 'I'm trying to undo the damage you may have caused yourself.'

Oh, God. He's not even concerned about himself. He's more concerned with my private pictures. He's more concerned with my *reputation than his own.*

Once again Pamsey felt like such a heel. She'd misjudged poor, gorgeous tech guy, Brett.

"Th-thank you," she said, quietly, humiliation stinging her heart. "By the way, I've finished the ad copy. It's still on my hard drive at home. I'll bring it first thing in the morning."

He nodded in acknowledgment but focused his dangerously sexy eyes back on the screen. Still, her body ached for his touch. She wanted more of Brett. Much, much more. How could he just give her a sneak preview of his delicious sexual power and leave her wanting more?

She had to fight the urge inside her right now to claim him. She wanted to push all the files off his desk and climb on the desk and tear off his shirt and tie and his suit. She wanted to feel his soft, firm hands on her naked body. She wanted him to do that magic sucking of her lips with his again and rekindle that sweet feeling of passionate heat she'd felt moments ago when he'd pressed his warm lips to hers. To taste that sweet minty taste of his mouth.

Would he touch her again? What would become of their relationship at the office? Would she ever know what it would be like to be in bed with Brett? She didn't think he would make a great lover—she knew it! From that kiss, that had her body and mind spinning—anticipation raced through her of what it would feel like to make love with Brett. The whole situation seemed so surreal.

Brett kissed me.

Her lips still tingled with delight. Her body was still under heightened arousal waiting for more, craving for more of Brett's magic touch.

All her life, Pamsey had been the careful one. Never showing her feelings much. Playing it safe at the office. She didn't have much of a life outside of work, except taking good care of her mom—which she felt was a great honor. She loved her mother more than anything in this world.

As Brett continued to focus on deleting her email message from the inboxes on the server, she wondered if he was thinking about her, too—or what just transpired between them.

Did he even carry a condom on him—just in case? God, she hoped so. Then again, it didn't look as if anything more would happen tonight between them, did it?

Damn it.

Just then the lyrics "Ain't too proud to beg" climbed into her mind and stayed there, refusing to leave.

Stop it, Pamsey. You will not be begging this sexy geek god to make love to you tonight. No matter how badly you want him.

She glanced around his office and was impressed with all the awards he'd won, displayed on the wall.

She got up, leaving him to his work, afraid to disturb him in case he missed something and the email inadvertently becomes read by everyone.

She noted a few pictures on the wall of Brett with a group of young adults in wheel chairs.

Why haven't I seen this before?

Brett wore a T-shirt like the rest of the team. It read: Champion of Hope Winners. Her heart melted.

The picture was taken outside of a lavish and extravagant mansion of some sort with a beautiful water fountain in the front.

That couldn't possibly be Brett's home, could it?

Brett rarely talked about himself at the office or what he did in his spare time. There were countless small pictures in the frame of Brett with kids in a camp-like setting. He seemed to be some sort of coach.

Her heart melted and she felt a squeeze center in her chest.

Brett was really a cool guy. She'd misjudged him. But damn it. Why didn't the guy talk about himself?

Just then...Brett lowered the lights in his office by remote control.

The office was now dim, save for the bright light from the computer screen.

"Because I don't feel the need to always talk about myself."

"What?" Pamsey spun her head around in shock. Did he read minds, too?

"Isn't that what you were thinking? I can read your mind," he said.

Her jaw fell open.

"Not literally, Pamsey. I could read the expression on your face," he said, standing up, his hands shoved in his pants pockets.

"I thought you were still deleting the messages. So you were watching me?" She arched a brow.

"I'm always watching you, Pamsey," he said in a low voice and she melted under the heat of his dark, sexy gaze.

"You are?"

"Yes," he said, seductively. His warm eyes penetrated her.

" I...I don't understand."

"What's there to understand?" he said, inching closer to her again and the air around her thickened with erotic tension...

Chapter 11

Pamsey's heart palpitated. "You said you're always watching me," she whispered, her body feeling numb with excitement.

"From the day you started your orientation here at TLC. The way you changed your hair color every four months...And changed your style of dressing when you got promoted. God, I love when you wear that black pencil skirt with the white blouse."

"What?" she said, softly. Her ex-fiancé never noticed things like her hairstyle changes or cared what she was wearing.

"You're the most beautiful woman I've ever met, inside and out," he murmured, stroking her chin with his finger again sending shivers of delight down her spine. She leaned against the counter by the wall display, facing him. "You have no idea what you've done to me over the years. I've always wanted you, Pamsey."

"You have?" she said, breathless with disbelief.

Had Brett noticed all those things about her this whole time? And there she thought he never even knew she was alive.

Her lips trembled with anticipation. They were so close to his again and she could not contain herself.

"I...I thought you didn't even notice me. You never let on," she breathed.

"You were off limits," he said, his soft lips brushing hers so sweetly again, caressing her flesh, "and you still are," he said, his voice hoarse.

"No, I'm not," she murmured between his hot kisses. His lips slid down to her cheek and over to her ear where he sucked and nipped her earlobe. She felt dizzy with ecstasy.

"Oh, God," she cried out. His touch was so sexually-charged. Her inner thighs were dripping wet right now. What would he think of her, if he knew just how much he turned her on and spun her senses into overdrive?

"Yes," he breathed between seducing her, kissing her gently, "you are. Off. Limits."

His lips moved lower down to the sensitive flesh on her neck and he squeezed her with his lips, sucking her sensuously and devouring her flesh as she breathed harder and harder, feeling her inner thighs throb harder and harder.

"But I want you, Brett," she whispered, breathlessly as he caressed her neck with his sweet lips. "Please, I want you now..."

"Oh, Pamsey," he said, sliding his hand down her back then further down squeezing her ass. She jolted with delight, relishing in the warmth of Brett's intimate touch. He continued to shower her with soft, passionate kisses on her flesh and moved his hand then slid off her tank top. Her breasts were exposed, her nipples tightened harder under the coolness of the office air conditioner.

"God, you're so beautiful," he groaned, his lips curled in approval while his eyes captured her naked breasts as if they were the most beautiful things he'd ever seen. Seductively, he lowered his head to her bosom, massaging one breast while his mouth sweetly covered her other, sucking on her hard nipple, his tongue sliding across her peak while she arched her back on the counter, moaning in pleasure.

"Oh," she cried out, breathing hard and fast. Brett was so...good with his tongue, with his lips.

She leaned back on the counter as Brett moved his other hand at the hemline of her skirt and carefully slid it up and gently caressed her wet and warm throbbing folds.

"Oh, you're so wet, it's driving me crazy," he growled while stroking her gently until she tingled all over her body. "Is this what you like?" he said in a low, hoarse voice, a wicked grin on his lips.

She nodded, moaning in delight, her body's senses heightened by his silky touch as tingles spiraled up and down her body.

A surge of heat raced through Pamsey. Her heartbeat sped as Brett lowered his head down on her, stroking her wetness first with his fingers through her panties, then he moved the silky fabric of her underwear to the side, her folds fully exposed. A wicked grin curled his lips before he softly slid his tongue inside then kissed and sucked on her warm flesh.

Pamsey closed her eyes and arched her back in ecstasy, spreading her legs while Brett tasted her sex. His lips were soft and caressing.

The intimate moment between them blew her mind. She could not have possibly imagined Brett so close to her nakedness the way he was—before now.

"Turn around," he said, in a hoarse voice, getting up.

She did what he asked, anticipation overwhelming her.

She spread her hands on the counter. He kissed the back of her neck so sensuously.

Damn! Where did he learn to kiss like that?

He then slid his hand over her breasts, teasing and squeezing her taut nipple, one at a time, sending shivers of delight dancing through her body.

His mouth moved to the side of her neck, nipping on her sensitive flesh while she moaned in her throat, overcome with the erotic sensation, the delicious scent of his cologne and the warmth of his breath on her skin.

He then lowered himself on her from behind. Her heart hammered hard in her chest. Her spine tingled. Intense heat burned inside her.

"Your ass is more beautiful in the flesh," he growled.

Heat rushed to her cheeks.

He caressed her buttocks, and her inner thighs pulsed hard.

He then moved down on her and slid his hands to her front from behind, caressing her swollen folds again as she groaned with pleasure, arching her back. He then slid his tongue over her front from behind, sucking on her folds and caressing her to ecstasy.

"Oh, oh, Brett," she cried out as she came hard and fast, while his mouth kissed her sex.

Her orgasm was intense and explosive. Her body trembled with sweet electrical pulses as waves of intense heat shot through her.

Breathing hard, Pamsey's body became flimsy, her legs weak, Brett held her and hugged her, kissing her passionately.

"You really turn me on, Pamsey. You're so beautiful." He growled, kissing her shoulder blade then moving his lips to her neck. She leaned back into him, feeling his hard erection from behind. The scent of his sweet cologne intoxicated her.

She wanted so badly to cover his erection with her mouth. She wanted to taste Brett's sex.

She then licked her lips and unzipped his expensive dress pants. She couldn't wait to free his hard erection. Her eyes opened wide when she saw how *huge* he was. Her heart raced like mad in her chest.

He was well endowed. She lowered her head to his mid section as he leaned against the desk. At first she, stroked his hard length and then she slowly wrapped her lips around him taking him in fully as he groaned with pleasure.

The sound of his moans turned her on even more. He tasted like clean like soap. She moved back and forth on him taking him in deeper and deeper as he held onto her head.

"Oh, Pamsey, I'm going to come," he growled in his low sexy deep voice.

He stopped her before anything happened, leaving her breathless.

"I've got a condom," he said, breathless. "You want to go all the way?"

"Yes," she moaned, kissing him tenderly. "Yes, now..."

A surge of desire drove through her. She'd waited for this moment for years. She'd wanted him since she'd first started working for him and with him years ago at the company, she didn't want to wait any longer.

Thank heavens he had a condom with him or she'd go insane!

He reached into his pocket and took out a golden foil square packet and ripped it open with his teeth. He rolled on the rubber over his huge thick length in no time.

"Come here, baby," he moaned, gently tugging her to him.

"Can we do it, standing up?"

He grinned. "I can do it anyway you like, beautiful."

"Yes," she said, "I like the sound of that." She got up on the desk and sat with her legs spread apart. Brett leaned into her and slowly kissed the base of her neck as she arched back, her arms wrapped around him.

He held her gaze sensuously, breathing deeply as he slowly placed his erection at her folds, tantalizing her. He then moved his hips and slowly slid deep inside her as she gasped with delight, tightening around his shaft. He pulled out slowly, leaving her body tingling. He then went inside her again deeper and deeper this time as she squeezed around him, accommodating him.

"Oh, you're so tight, baby." His groaning intensified her arousal.

He then started moving his manhood faster inside her and penetrating her hard and firm, back and forth in rhythmic motion as she shook on the desk, crying out his name. Her nails dug into his strong muscular shoulder blades.

She cried out his name again as a delicious sensation shook her body. The intense orgasm left her breathless, shaken as the heat of electricity pulsed through her.

Waves of intense heat surged inside her.

She was breathless. He came soon after her, groaning in pleasure, thrusting hard and fast between her legs. Then...

They both collapsed on the desk together, panting as they melted into each other's arms.

Chapter 12

"You're amazing, you know that?" Brett sighed heavily, moments later.

"So are you?" Her lips curved into a sated grin as she snuggled into his muscular chest.

There was a brief pause.

"You know there was something you wrote that really got to me in your diary," Brett said as they hugged each other in the office, the lights off save for a dim light on his desk.

"What is it?" she asked curiously, as her heart pulsed faster.

"I've never met a woman who had so much in common with me. We both like the same things. The same foods, the same choice in music."

"I know! I *love* classical music. That's all I ever listen to. People think I'm nuts."

"You're not nuts. *They* are," he said with a grin. "You're brilliant. It takes a special person to appreciate the classics."

"Thanks."

"And the magical miracle of the universe," he said, kissing her intermittently as he continued to make out with her.

"Oh, that," she moaned, "You mean like looking up at the stars at night?" her breathless voice trailed off.

"Can't believe you share the same interests and appreciation as me. My ex never understood that. I'd always try to get her to slow down and appreciate the things we take for granted."

"She didn't deserve you, Brett."

He gently pulled her closer to him and their lips sweetly entwined. They kissed each other like long-lost lovers, with intense passion. She couldn't wait to pleasure Brett again. Her body was still buzzing. She didn't think she could ever come down from her erotic high.

She heard a loud ping from the computer on his desk.

Another email?

Brett looked across the room at the screen, his jaw clenched. Could he see from that distance? The man had twenty-twenty vision. Clearly, he was peeved. Brett pulled himself away from her again, leaving her breathless.

"What is it?" she said, panting, fixing her clothes. She felt as if her head was spinning out of control right now.

"I'm taking you home."

"What? Now? But..."

"I've broken company rules, Pamsey. Let's pretend this never happened. I shouldn't have done that—not here."

Pamsey felt stung.

Let's pretend this didn't happen?

"Don't bother. I drove here." Her tone was clipped and icy cold.

"No, you didn't. You took a cab. I saw the security camera."

"Why are you doing this, Brett?" She wanted to say 'don't you want me, too?' but the last thing she wanted to sound was desperate. Even if she was desperate for him to take her right there again in the office in the middle of the night.

Oh, if HR could see them now. Neither of them would be working for the company tomorrow, if that were the case. But she badly needed this job. And she knew how much Brett cared about his position at the company—even though he seemed well off enough not to ever need to work.

Brett then stroked her chin with his finger and she shivered.

"Because, we've just broken company policy."

"Brett, you're driving me crazy. I hate you."

"Funny, that's not what you said a moment ago." His boyish grin almost got the best of her.

She heaved a sigh.

"We have an important meeting, Pamsey. A rep from B&B will be in the office in the morning to discuss their upcoming campaign." He looked again at the computer screen.

"But what are we going to do about us?"

His sexy gaze captured hers hungrily. "I'll work something out for us."

Pamsey swallowed hard. She resisted the urge to lick her lips. Her heart galloped hard in her chest. She didn't know what got to her but just the way he said it in his silky voice heated up her arousal to an all-time high. She was conscious of her heavy breathing.

She could not believe she'd been so intimate with Brett Lorenz, CEO of TLC Advertising.

One night with Brett and she wasn't able to think straight.

The truth was, right now, she couldn't think straight and they hadn't even finished what they started. She was tempted to look at the email he'd just been sent but she dared not.

"And I have to come back to the office after I take you home."

"Why do you have to come back here?" She bit down on her lip, trying to hide the pain of her disappointment.

"I have some B&B files to go through. I'm not done looking over some discrepancies."

"I see. Don't you ever sleep?"

"Not much." He paused for a moment.

"Well you know that saying," she said, "'Early to bed, early to rise, makes a man healthy, wealthy, and wise.'"

"I'll keep that in mind," he said.

Pamsey glanced at the photo on the wall. "If I had a place like that, I'd be sleeping there a lot." She was half-joking but she was surprised at his answer.

"Well, if I had someone like you to wake up with every morning, maybe I would be motivated to sleep there more."

She grinned at his warm sentiment. Her heart thrashed about in her chest. So that was his home? Was he insane? How could he not want to stay there often?

"I'm surprised you work for a living. You look like you live in a palace."

"I shared the home with my ex-fiancée."

Her stomach fell. "You did?"

"Yes, but I found out that while I was working late at the office, she was bringing in her lover through the back door."

"Oh, no."

"I confronted her about it. There are security cameras set up outside the home. Anyway, long story short, she got pregnant and it wasn't for me."

"Sorry to hear that. What happened after that?"

"She'd sent me a text telling me she was going to be with him. I never forgave Rhea for that. I noticed from your...diary notes that I happened to come across that your boyfriend left you for a girl named Rhea. Seems like quite a coincidence."

"Yeah, my ex Caleb was a jerk. He sent me a private message on Twitter breaking off our engagement."

"Caleb? Did you say his name's Caleb?"

"Yes, why?"

"Well, isn't that something."

"Wait a minute. Please don't' tell me that..." She quickly typed in the URL for Facebook then went to Caleb's profile. Sure enough, there was a picture on the screen of Caleb and his new wife.

Brett glanced at the screen. "Looks like your ex and my ex are together."

"Well, I'll be damned."

"No, beautiful," he said, stroking her chin with his finger. "You'll *never* be damned. You are so beautifully blessed in so many ways. And I'm going to make sure that no one hurts you like that again."

His words sent a wave of intense heat sliding over her. He really meant that, didn't he?

"Is that a promise?"

"That's a promise I intend to keep. You are way too beautiful and sweet to be hurt like that. I had no idea you felt the way you did about me the way I feel about you until I read your notes. I'm never going to let something so good like that go. It's not every day you meet someone who feels the same way about you."

She swallowed hard. "That's true. I had no idea that Caleb was secretly looking for another relationship when we were together."

"Real men never go into another relationship while they're still in one."

An appreciative smile curved her lips. "Where were you all my life?"

"Right here, working with you in the same office." A cheeky grin curved his lips.

"I guess TLC should look into revising their workplace dating policies."

He shook his head. "They might not feel the same way. Anyway, I think our exes deserve to be with each other."

"Could you imagine what they'd think if they knew we were together? That is way too funny."

He grinned. A sexy dimple surfaced on his handsome face. Then his expression changed slightly.

"We have an important meeting tomorrow—or later this morning," he said, correcting himself and noting the time.

"Right, of course. And I'll make sure to send the *correct* file."

A charming grin played on his soft sweet lips.

"Why don't you come home with me," he whispered softly.

The way his sexy gaze locked with hers stirred a delicious reaction in her body.

"I wish I could but...my mother's at home, she needs me. I need to relieve the caregiver from the agency," she murmured, grinning.

"You're mother's lucky to have a daughter like you."

She gushed.

"Well, maybe it's for the best. I don't think I'll be able to control myself if I take you home tonight. I'd keep making love to you right into the morning...and probably not go into work later in the morning," he said, in a silky deep voice.

Surprise caught her off guard. Her heart pumped hard and fast as it hammered against her ribcage.

Pamsey could not breathe.

It was one o'clock in the morning—and they were still at the office.

A grin curved his sexy lips. "It's officially Friday, February the fourteenth."

"Valentine's Day. I know," she said quietly while her heart pounded loud and forceful in her chest.

"You know I used to hate Valentine's Day since Rhea broke off with me on that day."

"That was an awful thing to do."

"I'm over it now. Valentine's means something more to me now."

"It does?"

"Yes. And thanks to you, it means something beautiful again." He gently brushed his lips against hers again, sucking on her lower lip and caressing her. Waves of pleasure rolled through her.

"Same here," she said. "Oh, but what about the policy on dating in the workplace at TLC? We're in violation of the rules." She frowned.

"I think some rules are meant to be broken—if there's a good reason."

A feeling of warmth centered in her heart. She'd never felt so desired as she did now.

"But for now, let's just keep this between us and I'll make sure that Lee's new monitoring of office supplies doesn't include secret hidden cameras in these offices."

Pamsey's eyes opened wide. She felt her lungs squeeze. "God, I hope not."

"Relax, beautiful. I'll talk with Lee in the morning. I have a few things I need to straighten out with her."

He then leaned in closer to her, recapturing her lips as he pressed his sweet lips to hers again, as waves of intense pleasure swept through her body.

The day and evening turned out to be full of unexpected surprises.

So it was true then that some disasters could lead to blessings in disguise when you're with the right person.

Pamsey had a strange feeling things would *never* be the same again at the TLC office.

And for the first time in a while, she was actually looking forward to going into work every day.

* * *

Books by Shadonna Richards
THE BELMONT FAMILY / BILLIONAIRES OF BELMONT
The Billionaire's Bride for a Day (Dane & Olivia)
The Billionaire's Promise (Brandon & Faith)
The Billionaire's Housekeeper (Chase & Abbi)
The Billionaire's Lost & Found Love (Cole & Hope)
The Billionaire's Redemption (Leo & Honesty)

THE ROMERO BROTHERS
The Billionaire's Second-Chance Bride, #1 (Antonio III & Lucy)
A Bride for the Billionaire Bad Boy, #2 (Lucas & Maxine)
The Playboy Billionaire, #3 (Zack & Blue)
The Billionaire's Island Romance, #3.5 (Christian & Arianna)
The Billionaire's Proposition, #4 (Carl & Venus)
The Billionaire's Baby, #5 (Jules & Amber)
The Billionaire's Assistant, #6 (Dion & Jenna-Lynn)
Snowbound with the Billionaire, #7 (Troy & Pamela)
The Billionaire's Marriage Proposal, #8 (Alonso & Britney)
THE BRIDE SERIES
An Unexpected Bride, #1 (Emma Wiggins & Evan Fletcher)
The Jilted Bride, #2 (Jody Anders & Jake Anderson)
The Matchmaker Bride, #3 (Sophie Wilson & Carlos Bradley III)

His Island Bride (Free), #4 (Jessica Mills & James Carrington)

An Unexpected Baby, #5 (The sequel to An Unexpected Bride)

WHIRLWIND ROMANCE SERIES

Accidentally Flirting with the CEO (Free) (Alexa Worthington & Jess Tandon)

Accidentally Married to the Billionaire (Kira Watson & Alessandro Romano)

Accidentally Falling for the Tycoon (Jen Anne Somers & Blake Harrington)

Accidentally Flirting with the CEO 2 (Alexa & Jess Tandon)

Accidentally Flirting with the CEO 3 (Alexa & Jess Tandon)

Accidentally Flirting with the CEO 4 (Pamsey Jackson & Brett Lorenz)

ABOUT THE AUTHOR

SHADONNA RICHARDS is a *USA Today* bestselling author who enjoys reading and writing about the magic of romance and the power of love. She has written more than 100 books and is the author of over 25 contemporary romance novels including books from The Bride Series, The Romero Brothers, Whirlwind Romance, and Billionaires of Belmont. Additionally, she wrote the non-fiction books A Gift of Hope, Count Your Blessings, and Think & Be Happy. She has over 500,000 downloads of her ebooks. Born in London, England, she has a B.A. Degree in Psychology.

Winner of Harlequin's So You Think You Can Write 2010 Day Two Challenge, she believes in the importance of promoting literacy. She's a proud mommy and lives with her husband and son.

AUTHOR CONTACT:

Email: shadonna@ymail.com

Website: www.shadonnarichards.blogspot.com

Facebook: www.facebook.com/authorshadonnarichards